HELLO, I'm THEA!

I'm *Geronimo Stilton*'s sister. As I'm sure you know from my brother's bestselling novels, I'm a special correspondent for *The Rodent's Gazette*, Mouse Island's most famous newspaper. Unlike my 'fraidy mouse brother, I absolutely adore traveling, having adventures, and meeting rodents from all around the world!

The adventure I want to tell you about begins at Mouseford Academy, the school I went to when I was a young mouseling. I had such a great experience there as a student that I came back to teach a journalism class.

When I returned as a grown mouse, I met five really special students: Colette, Nicky, Pamela, Paulina, and Violet. You could hardly imagine five more different mouselings, but they became great friends right away. And they liked me so much that they decided to name their group after me: the Thea Sisters! I was so touched by that, I decided to write about their adventures. So turn the page to read a fabumouse adventure about the

THEA SiSTERS!

Name: Nicky
Nickname: Nic
Home: Australia
Secret ambition: Wants to be an ecologist.
Loves: Open spaces and nature.
Strengths: She is always in a good mood, as long as she's outdoors!
Weaknesses: She can't sit still!
Secret: Nicky is claustrophobic — she can't stand being in small, tight places.

Nicky

Nicky

COLETTE

Name: Colette

Nickname: It's Colette, please. (She can't stand nicknames.)

Home: France

Secret ambition: Colette is very particular about her appearance. She wants to be a fashion writer.

Loves: The color pink.

Strengths: She's energetic and full of great ideas.

Weaknesses: She's always late!

Secret: To relax, there's nothing Colette likes more than a manicure and pedicure.

Colette

Name: Violet
Nickname: Vi
Home: China
Secret ambition: Wants to become a great violinist.
Loves: Books! She is a real intellectual, just like my brother, Geronimo.
Strengths: She's detail-oriented and always open to new things.
Weaknesses: She is a bit sensitive and can't stand being teased. And if she doesn't get enough sleep, she can be a real grouch!
Secret: She likes to unwind by listening to classical music and drinking green tea.

Violet

Name: Paulina
Nickname: Polly
Home: Peru
Secret ambition: Wants to be a scientist.
Loves: Traveling and meeting people from all over the world. She is also very close to her sister, Maria.
Strengths: Loves helping other rodents.
Weaknesses: She's shy and can be a bit clumsy.
Secret: She is a computer genius!

PAULINA

PAULINA

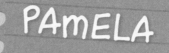

Name: Pamela
Nickname: Pam
Home: Tanzania
Secret ambition: Wants to become a sports journalist or a car mechanic.
Loves: Pizza, pizza, and more pizza! She'd eat pizza for breakfast if she could.
Strengths: She is a peacemaker. She can't stand arguments.
Weaknesses: She is very impulsive.
Secret: Give her a screwdriver and any mechanical problem will be solved!

Pamela

Geronimo Stilton

Thea Stilton
AND THE
BLUE SCARAB HUNT

Scholastic Inc.

New York   Toronto   London   Auckland
Sydney   Mexico City   New Delhi   Hong Kong

ISBN 978-0-545-34104-2

Copyright © 2009 by Edizioni Piemme S.p.A., Via Tiziano 32, 20145 Milan, Italy.

International Rights © Atlantyca S.p.A.

English translation © 2012 by Atlantyca S.p.A.

Based on an original idea by Elisabetta Dami.
www.geronimostilton.com

Published by Scholastic Inc., 557 Broadway, New York, NY 10012.
SCHOLASTIC and associated logos are trademarks and/or registered trademarks of Scholastic Inc.

Stilton is the name of a famous English cheese. It is a registered trademark of the Stilton Cheese Makers' Association. For more information, go to www.stiltoncheese.com.

Text by Thea Stilton
Original title *Caccia allo scarabeo blu*
Cover by Arianna Rea (pencils), Daniela Geremia (inks), and Ketty Formaggio (color)
Illustrations by Francesco Bisaro, Jacopo Brandi, Elisa Falcone, Paolo Ferrante, Michela Frare, Daniela Geremia, Yoko Ippolitoni, Rosa La Barbera, Roberta Pierpaoli, Arianna Rea, Maurizio Roggerone, and Roberta Tedeschi
Color by Alessandra Bracaglia, Ketty Formaggio, Elena Sanjust, and Micaela Tangorra
Graphics by Paola Cantoni with Michela Battaglin

Special thanks to Beth Dunfey
Translated by Emily Clement
Interior design by Kay Petronio

18   18/0

Printed in the U.S.A.   40
First printing, June 2012

IN FLIGHT
WITH MARIA

I love to TRAVEL around the world! My name is Thea Stilton, and I'm a **special** correspondent for *The Rodent's Gazette*, the newspaper run by my brother, Geronimo. The absolute best part of my job is getting to **SEE** new places! I've traveled practically everywhere on the planet, from Azerbaijan to Zimbabwe.

But today was a little different from most days. I was traveling for a truly **SPECIAL** occasion. I was on board a direct flight to Egypt, and

LUXOR

Luxor (al-Uqsur) is the modern name for the ancient city of Thebes, which was one of the most important religious centers in Egypt during the time of the pharaohs.

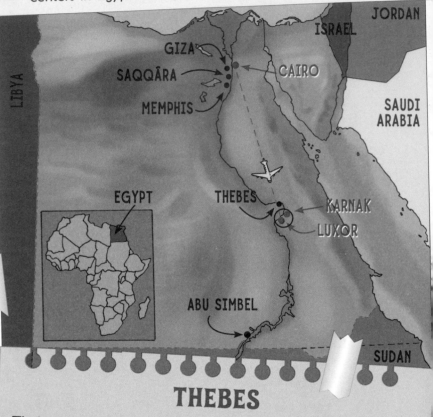

THEBES

Thebes was the capital of Egypt for many centuries. The Egyptian name was Waset, which means "the powerful." The name Thebes is Greek.

Today the only remaining parts of ancient Thebes on the right (east) bank of the Nile are the temples of Karnak and Luxor. The Valley of the Queens and the Valley of the Kings stretch along the left (west) bank. That's where the tombs of many pharaohs have been found.

seated next to me was a sweet little eight-year-old **mouſelet** from PERU!

If she looks familiar, that's probably because you've met her before. It's Maria, Paulina's little sister!* We were going to Luxor together to join PAULINA and the other Thea Sisters.

I'm sure you know all about the **THEA SiSTERS**. A little while back, I was invited to teach a class in adventure journalism at my old school, **MOUSEFORD ACADEMY**. Colette, nicky, PAMELA, PAULINA, and **Violet** — the Thea Sisters — were in my class. Without a doubt, they are the five brightest young rodents I've ever met!

Now, I'm sure you're wondering why I had to meet them in Luxor, and why I was traveling there with **Maria**. Well, you see, the Thea Sisters had made an extraordinary

---

* We met Maria during the Thea Sisters' adventure in Peru. You can read about it in my book *Thea Stilton and the Secret City*.

EGYPTOLOGY

Around 3000 BC, one of the world's richest and most fascinating civilizations — Egypt — began developing along the banks of the Nile River. Egyptology is the study of the language, history, and culture of this grand civilization.

EXTRAORDINARY MONUMENTS

The ancient Egyptians created some truly amazing monuments: the pyramids; the Great Sphinx in Giza; the temples of Karnak, Luxor, and Abu Simbel; the tombs of the pharaohs in the Valley of the Kings and the Valley of the Queens . . . The list goes on and on. To this day, we still aren't sure how the ancient Egyptians were able to build these massive structures with the limited tools available at the time.

THE PYRAMIDS OF KHUFU, KHAFRE, AND MENKAURE IN GIZA

ONE OF THE TWO TEMPLE OF ABU SIMBEL

OF ANCIENT EGYPT

BURIED WONDERS

No one knows how many other treasures await discovery in Egypt. Many works of art and valuable artifacts are still hidden beneath the desert sands. Unearthing them is a difficult and delicate process. Only archaeological experts can do it without the risk of harming these artifacts forever.

ANCIENT ANTITHEFT DEVICES

Throughout history, archaeological discoveries have attracted treasure hunters. Even in the time of the pharaohs, thieves sneaked into the monuments to steal the valuables kept there. For this reason, many speculate about the measures taken to protect the entrances to the most important ancient monuments.

THE TEMPLE OF HATSHEPSUT

THE GREAT SPHINX IN GIZA

aRchaeolOgical discovery during a trip to Egypt. I offered to write an article about the exhibition dedicated to their find. As for Maria, she was to be the guest of honor. Why? Keep reading and you'll soon find out!

I couldn't wait to listen to Colette, Pamela, Paulina, Violet, and Nicky tell me all about their latest adventure. Right now, I only had the headline — that the five mouselets had saved an ancient treasure from a band of TOMB RAIDERS! I was as eager for the full story as a bookmouse waiting for the final installment of *Ratty Potter.* I'll bet you are, too!

A story this fascinating was destined to become the subject of a good BOOK — a book that I had already decided to call *The Blue Scarab Hunt!*

THE GREATEST TREASURE in EGYPT!

Our story begins many months earlier, at **MOUSEFORD ACADEMY**. It was a chilly, gray winter day, and the history professor, Bartholomew Sparkle, was holding a SPECIAL class devoted to his upcoming **expedition** to Egypt.

Bartholomew Sparkle

"I have been invited by a **FAMOUSE** Egyptologist,* Professor Marcus Mouserson, to join his team of archaeologists!" Professor Sparkle told his students **solemnly**.

"Will you be there for a long time, Professor?" asked Paulina. She was very **INTERESTED** in ancient civilizations.

"I asked for a year off," the professor replied. "It's a great opportunity! I'm going to participate in an archaeological **dig** near the ancient city of Thebes. That's where Professor Mouserson is leading a group of *scholars* who are trying to bring the famous **TREASURE OF THE SUN** to **LiGHT**."

The professor turned on his trusty slide projector. An image of an ancient pyramid appeared on the screen. "You see, mouselets, since **PREHiSTORiC** times, mousekind has witnessed the continuous alternation of day

* An *Egyptologist* is a scholar who studies the civilization of ancient Egypt.

and night. By that I mean that day always follows night, with the rising and the setting of the **SUN**. But ancient rodents weren't able to explain this phenomenon **scientifically**, so they explained it in their own way."

From the back row came the squeak of Marcos Papatopos, a Greek student who had just entered the academy. "The ancient Greeks believed that the sun was a god, Helios, who **DROVE** a chariot of **FIRE** pulled by horses!"

"Exactly!" confirmed the professor, **delighted**. "The ancient Egyptians, on the other paw, believed the sun sailed through the sky on board a **ship**."

"Was the sun a god for the

THE NILE VALLEY

In the time of the pharaohs, Egyptian civilization spread across the green valley surrounding the Nile River, which was bordered by the desert on both sides. People lived in the valley because the river made the soil fertile.

ABU SIMBEL

THEBES
MOUNTAINS

ELEPHANTINE

IDFU

ASWÂN

KAWM UMBU

THEBES

The Nile crossed the entire civilization. Since the river was their major water source and the best way to reach the sea, it was an important landmark for the ancient Egyptians.

Egyptians, too?" Pamela asked.

"Yes, Pam! The most important **god**!" Professor Sparkle replied. "So **IMPORTANT** that it was given a different name for every phase of the day. The god Khepri took the form of a **scarab**, or beetle, and represented the **rising** sun."

"A scarab?! Gross!" Pamela **shivered**, **wrinkling** her nose. "Insects creep me out!"

"**Shhh!**" Violet hissed. She was so fascinated by the professor's lecture she didn't want to miss a squeak.

"The god Ra was the **sun** during the day, when it was bright and warm, while the god Atum-Ra was the sun at **sunset**," Professor Sparkle continued. "There's a legend about a pharaoh who built a **beautiful** temple to the sun gods. The ruins have never been discovered, but Professor Mouserson is convinced that the temple is out there. And he wants to be the one to unearth it!"

"Is that temple related to the TREASURE OF THE SUN?" asked Colette.

Professor Sparkle **nodded**. "Yes it is. Some papyruses say that the Treasure of the Sun, which was an offering to the god Ra,

PHARAOHS

The name *pharaoh* comes from the Egyptian *per 'aa,* which means "great house" or "palace." Over time, the word came to be used as the title of the king. The pharaoh had absolute power over his subjects and was worshiped as a god. One of the most important and famous pharaohs was Ramses II.

RAMSES II

was hidden in a **SECRET** place within the temple, but no one knows where. It is believed that the treasure is a vessel made of gold and filled with **precious** objects. It's supposed to be the greatest treasure in all of Egypt!"

"**OOOOOOOOOOOOH!**" the students sighed. They were enthralled by Professor Sparkle's tale.

"It's like something out of *Mousiana Jones and the Kingdom of the Rodent's Snout*," sighed Pam.

"So you're going to search for the treasure, Professor? **WOW!**" said Nicky, impressed.

The professor **smiled**, and his eyes shined with **EXCITEMENT**. "That's right! I'm on the hunt for a treasure of enormouse value. If we find it, it will reveal new secrets about the great Egyptian civilization!"

THE BLUE SCARAB

The **mouselings** learned that many archaeologists had searched for the Treasure of the Sun, but no one had ever succeeded in finding it. Some experts had come to believe that the treasure was just a myth — that it didn't really exist. But that had **changed** after an important discovery Professor Mouserson had made two years earlier.

Professor Sparkle **clicked** through the slides until he reached one that showed a **beautiful** blue scarab. "When he dug inside the famouse **temple** in Karnak, Professor Mouserson unearthed a papyrus and a **PRECIOUS** scarab made of lapis lazuli. They were inside a sealed

terra-cotta container."

The next slide appeared on the screen. It showed the scarab **turned** over on its back. Strange symbols were carved on its stomach. Professor Sparkle pointed to these symbols. "Mouserson has translated the hieroglyphs* on the scarab and the papyrus. It's hard to decipher their exact meaning, but they seem to contain clues to the location of the pharaoh's temple. And they even mention the secret room that holds the Treasure of the Sun. We're very close to the **discovery** of the century!

"For an expedition like this, we'll need all the **HELP** we can get," the professor concluded. "So we're offering you the chance to participate in the **dig** during spring break!"

A wave of excitement rippled through the

---

* *Hieroglyphs* are symbols that the ancient Egyptians used to write.

students: Could they really go to **Egypt**?!

"The dig site is very isolated," the professor warned them. "You'll have to live in a tent and adapt to the **WEATHER**! But the work won't be too hard. You'll help us by cataloging the objects we find."

Five paws **SNAPPED** into the air as if they were all attached to the same spring. Whose five paws? Why, the Thea Sisters', of course!

ANCIENT EGYPT

The great Egyptian civilization emerged thanks to the **Nile River**, whose waters would rise once a year and flood the area around it, depositing silt, a mud that makes the earth very fertile. The ancient Egyptians called the land surrounding the Nile *kemet*, which means "black land" (the color of silt), while the desert that surrounded *kemet* came to be called *deshret*, or "red land."

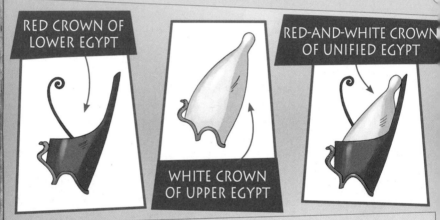

RED CROWN OF LOWER EGYPT

WHITE CROWN OF UPPER EGYPT

RED-AND-WHITE CROWN OF UNIFIED EGYPT

Originally, Egypt was divided into two lands: **Upper Egypt** and **Lower Egypt**. Lower Egypt consisted of the area in the north, near the Nile delta. Its symbol was a papyrus and its crown was red. Upper Egypt was the Nile Valley from Aswan to Heliopolis. Its symbol was a lotus and its crown was white.

In 3000 BC, Upper Egypt and Lower Egypt unified under the authority of a single pharaoh, called Ruler of the Two Lands. The two crowns were combined into one, known as the *pschent*, or "double crown."

Egyptian society had a very rigid structure. . . .

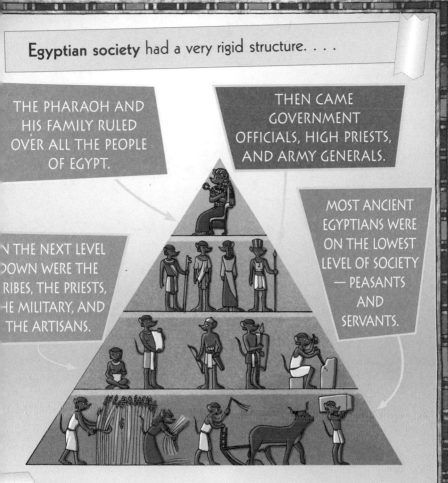

THE PHARAOH AND HIS FAMILY RULED OVER ALL THE PEOPLE OF EGYPT.

THEN CAME GOVERNMENT OFFICIALS, HIGH PRIESTS, AND ARMY GENERALS.

MOST ANCIENT EGYPTIANS WERE ON THE LOWEST LEVEL OF SOCIETY — PEASANTS AND SERVANTS.

N THE NEXT LEVEL DOWN WERE THE RIBES, THE PRIESTS, HE MILITARY, AND THE ARTISANS.

Scribes played a very important role in ancient Egypt. Since they knew how to read and write, when most people did not, the scribes became very powerful. In the most ancient times, scribes were chosen only from the members of the upper class. As time passed, other members of society were taught to write.

Actually, Colette's paw wouldn't have shot up if Pam hadn't grabbed her wrist and **raised** it for her.

"The desert?" Colette squeaked in protest. "It'll wreak havoc on my fur!"

"Come on, Coco!" Pam whispered back. "You can't pass this up! An opportunity like this is worth its weight in cheese."

Professor Sparkle *smiled* at his students' enthusiasm. The Thea Sisters didn't know it yet, but they'd just taken the first step toward an extraordinary new **ADVENTURE**!

A PLUNGE INTO THE PAST

Three months later, an airplane carrying the Thea Sisters landed at the international airport in Luxor. The flight had been **VERY LONG**, with a layover in Cairo and two additional stops. The mouselets were extremely **sleepy**.

It was almost as if the city knew how tired they were. It welcomed them with a warm evening and a beautiful blue sky.

"Well! This is a nice thank-you for our **EFFORT** to get here!" Paulina declared.

CAIRO

Cairo is the current capital of Egypt. It's a metropolis of about sixteen million people.

It's located on the banks of the Nile, close to the mouth of the river, but its edges extend into the desert and to Giza, where the most famous pyramids of Egypt stand.

Professor **Sparkle** was there waiting for them.

"Welcome to Egypt!" said the professor as he led them out of the airport.

The mouselets were **BURNING** with eagerness to see the **dig**, but Professor Sparkle had other plans for them. He pointed to two **carriages** coming their way. "I

have a surprise for you!" he said. "This is the perfect time to admire the wonders of Luxor. These carriages will take us on a full tour of the temples!"

The five Thea Sisters cheered: It was a truly **FABUMOUSE** idea! They scampered into the carriages and made themselves comfortable.

They rumbled over wide **STREETS** lined with grand modern buildings. Then they passed through tiny, narrower streets lined with low white houses.

"I feel as if we've traveled back in time!" Nicky squeaked.

All of a sudden, the **illuminated** Temple of Luxor loomed in front of them. The mouselets could just barely make out two one-eyed statues of pharaohs in the darkness of the grand entrance. The pharaohs sat on their thrones, powerful and **MYSTERIOUS**.

The carriages circled around the obelisk* in the plaza, and a **wide**, straight street opened up before them. On each side was a long line of sphinxes. Their human faces were illuminated, while their lion bodies

---

* An *obelisk* is a monument similar to a column but with a square base and the point of a pyramid.

were lost in the SHADOWS of the night.

It made the Thea Sisters' jaws drop.
"**Cheesecake!**"

Professor Sparkle grinned. "No one can resist the wonders of ancient Egypt! This is the path of the sphinxes, which links the Temple of Luxor with the temples of Karnak. Imagine how amazing this place must have been in ancient times!"

Then he added in a **HURRIED** tone, "Now it's off to the hotel for sleep. Tomorrow morning we'll visit Karnak, and then we'll join the **archaeological dig**."

Violet couldn't believe her ears. "We'll be

THE SPHINX

In ancient Egypt, the sphinx was a creature with a lion's body and the head of a human — sometimes the likeness of a pharaoh. The Great Sphinx is located in Giza. It is the largest statue to survive from ancient times till the modern day, and stands about 240 feet long and 66 feet high.

visiting Karnak?! **Hooray!** I thought we had to join the dig as soon as possible."

The professor seemed **uncomfortable** talking about the dig. "Um, yes, that *was* the plan, but . . . you absolutely must see the temples of Karnak: They're marvemouse! In fact, I asked Professor Mouserson for a day off."

Colette noticed Professor Sparkle's **expression** grow **SERIOUS** when he mentioned the famouse Egyptologist.

CLUE! "Is Professor Mouserson very strict?" Colette asked **nervously**. "He's a **TYRANT**!" Professor Sparkle burst out. But then he caught himself. "That is, he's very meticulous. At the dig, not even a mosquito **flies** by without his permission!"

Professor Sparkle seems nervous when he talks about Professor Mouserson. But why?

KHEPRI, THE SCARAB GOD

The next morning, glorious sunshine greeted the Thea Sisters the moment they woke up.

"Dress light, **mouselets**!" Nicky recommended. "It's already the middle of summer here. SPRING ended a long time ago!"

Colette stepped out onto the balcony. "I'll have to put on a double layer of sunblock to protect my fur from this intense **sunshine**!"

The mouselets laughed, but then they all followed her example. They spread **SUNBLOCK** all over their snouts, put on sunglasses, and covered their heads with large, colorful hats.

In the hotel lobby, they found Professor

Sparkle waiting for them. He was particularly **anxious**. It seemed like he was in a big hurry to get to Karnak!

"The first thing I need to do is take some measurements of the statue of the god Khepri," he explained to his **students**. "Then we'll visit the rest of the temple."

"The god Khepri is the scarab, right?" Pam recalled.

Professor Sparkle **CHUCKLED**. "I see that made an impression on you! **Ha ha ha!**" Then he added, "There's a huge pink **GRANITE** statue of Khepri in Karnak. Professor Mouserson found another scarab that resembles the **statue**. That's why I need to take measurements."

"That new **scarab** is a clue, right, Professor? If the professor has started to **dig** in that area, that must mean the Treasure of the Sun is hidden nearby," Paulina guessed.

Professor Sparkle's expression **DARKENED** at these words. "Maybe . . ."

He didn't say any more, because they had arrived at their destination. The professor **QUICKLY** scampered ahead, as if he already knew where to go.

Meanwhile, Violet turned to the other mouselets and read the guidebook she'd

KARNAK

Karnak is just north of Luxor. Its complex of temples is the largest in Egypt. An avenue of sphinxes with rams' heads connects the temple complex to the Nile River, while a second avenue of sphinxes with human heads connects the complex to the Temple of Luxor.

The most ancient part of this complex of temples was built in 2000 BC. In the years that followed, more and more temples were added.

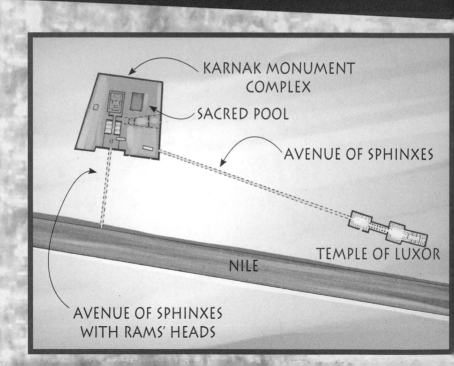

KARNAK MONUMENT COMPLEX

SACRED POOL

AVENUE OF SPHINXES

TEMPLE OF LUXOR

NILE

AVENUE OF SPHINXES WITH RAMS' HEADS

brought with her. "The ancient name for Karnak was Ipet-Isut, which means 'the holiest of places.' The Sacred Pool in Karnak was used for purification. During religious ceremonies, the ancient people would **submerge** small boats filled with statues of the different gods."

Pamela interrupted her, pointing to a spot ahead of them. "It's the scarab!" Then she **shook** her snout. "Ugh! I just don't see how anyone could worship a symbol of a creepy-crawly insect!" Pam hated **BUGS** of all shapes and sizes. They gave her the heebie-jeebies.

Paulina fished her camera out of her backpack. "Strike a pose, Pam! I'll snap a picture of you with your favorite Egyptian god! Ha ha ha!"

Meanwhile, Professor Sparkle was **FIDDLING**

with his camera tripod. "Could you give me a paw, mouselets?"

With Nicky's and Violet's **help**, the professor took extremely precise measurements of the **pink** granite scarab and the pedestal connected to it. He even consulted a compass. Then he recorded all the data in a notebook.

"Just as I thought!" he muttered to himself. As he squeaked, a photograph **SLIPPED** out of the notebook and onto the ground.

Pam picked it up. "Another scarab? Is this some kind of obsession, Professor?"

Curious, Colette drew closer to get a better look.

It was a group **PHOTO**. In the foreground was an old rodent who had a bossy expression and **bulging**

eyes that reminded Colette of a great big toad. But someone else caught her attention, too: a **young** female rodent standing next to Professor Sparkle.

"Who is this **mouselet**, Professor?" she asked.

"Oh, that's Dunya, Professor Mouserson's assistant," he answered, glancing at the photo. "And as you can see, that's the statue

of the scarab god, Khepri, here in Karnak."

"Fascinating," said Colette.

Paulina pointed at the **scarab** in the photo, curious. "Is this why you've been taking all these measurements, Professor? To **see** whether the scarab that Mouserson found is identical to this one?"

The professor didn't respond: He was lost in his **NOTES** again. "I knew it . . . Mouserson is digging in the **WRONG** place!" he mumbled.

The Thea Sisters looked at one another in **CONFUSION**. What did the professor mean? Was this why he wasn't in a hurry to return to the dig?

Professor Sparkle believes that Mouserson is digging in the wrong place! Why is he being so secretive about his investigations?

LOST IN THE LABYRINTH

The Thea Sisters had a thousand questions for their professor, but before they could squeak, a crowd of tourists in **brightly colored** clothes entered the courtyard surrounding the Sacred Pool. **Professor Sparkle** hastily packed up all his delicate instruments of **measurement**.

"Mouselets, let's get out of here before we **drown** in this crowd of tourists!"

He passed his bag to Colette. "Could you hold on to this until we get outside? I think I can **guide** you to the exit."

The mouselets followed him, careful not to lose him in the **LABYRINTH** of pillars, columns, gigantic statues, and crumbling walls.

As they entered a **LONG** corridor, the professor hissed, "Quickly! We're about to arrive in the grand hypostyle hall!"

He started walking faster, leaving the mouselets trailing behind. The Thea Sisters would have liked to stop and **admire** their surroundings, but they gave in and **scurried** after him.

At the **tail** end of the group, Violet tried to keep up while reading from her guidebook. "Okay, the hypostyle hall . . . Here it is! It

means 'supported by columns.' There are 134 colossal columns, and —"

BANG!

Violet tripped over a loose S T O N E, and Nicky, who was ahead of her, grabbed her before she ended up head over paws.

"Hey, are you okay, **Vi**?"

"I'm fine, thanks. But look over there!"

A short distance from them, they glimpsed

a small side room with walls covered in COLORFUL paintings.

"I think that's a picture of the Treasure of the Sun!" Violet exclaimed, pointing to one particular Painting. She peeked at her guidebook again. "Yes! It says so right here."

The picture showed a procession of rodents carrying a golden boat. The two mouselets stared at it in fascination.

Then they realized their friends were way ahead of them. When Nicky and Violet hurried out of the room, they couldn't see

OOOH!

anyone they knew. Their companions had disappeared!

"A few minutes of distraction and we're totally lost!" Violet moaned. "Now how will we FIND them? I feel like a rat in a maze!"

Nicky wasn't worried. She had a great sense of direction. "Don't get your tail in a twist, Violet! We'll find a way out."

With Nicky leading the way, the two mouselets scampered up and down corridors until they could see sunlight streaming through the gigantic columns.

"This must be the famouse hypostyle hall," Violet observed after checking the PHOTOGRAPHS in her guidebook. "Whew, what a crowd! There are more rodents here than at New Mouse City's annual CheeseFest. We'll never find our friends."

It's easy to get lost in this labyrinth!

STOOD UP!

Karnak's **ruins** are among the most beautiful and fascinating in all of Egypt, but they're also a real **labyrinth**!

The Thea Sisters spent a long, loooong time looking for one another amid the tourists who were **wandering** all over the place.

Finally, the five **friends** were reunited outside the temple of Amun-Ra, on a street lined with sphinxes with rams' heads.

The sun was still high in the sky, and the **HEAT** was stifling. Colette waved a **fan** back and forth to cool down, but it didn't help much. "Oof! It's hotter than grilled cheese, mouselets! Are we all here? Where's Professor Sparkle? As soon as we reached that room with the columns, I lost **SIGHT** of him."

Paulina took out her **cell phone**. "I lost him, too. Wait, I'll try to call him. He's got to be here somewhere."

She had barely finished her sentence when her phone beeped. She'd received a text message.

Nicky drew closer to Paulina and read aloud, "'Urgent business! Don't worry,

BE-BEEEP! BE-BEEEP!

just head back to the hotel. I'll be there soon. Bart.'"

The Thea Sisters were **ASTOUNDED**.

"Did he really sign it 'Bart'?!" Colette asked, bewildered. "Professor Sparkle has **NEVER** used that nickname before!"

Paulina read the message again. "'Urgent business'?! And this is right after he told us his **doubts** about Professor Mouserson's dig. What do you think it means?"

"I don't like it when someone tells me not to **worry**," Nicky said. "It always has the opposite effect on me."

Violet tried to calm her friends. "Oh, **mouselets**, my grandpa Chen always says, 'It's not strange for a strange mouse to

act strangely!'"

Her friends stared at her for a minute. Then they all started to laugh, which broke the **tension**.

Pam nodded. "You're right, Violet! The professor has been acting **STRANGELY** ever since we arrived. Let's go back to the hotel. Maybe we'll find him there already."

But they didn't find him. The mouselets **waited** the rest of the day for the professor to show up. They tried **AGAIN AND AGAIN** to reach him by cell phone, but he never answered. So the next morning at **BREAKFAST**, the Thea Sisters decided to do something about it.

CLUE!

Paulina started them off. "Sisters, we need to take **ACTION**! This story about

Why did Professor Sparkle leave the Thea Sisters? Was it because he'd discovered that Professor Mouserson's expedition was digging in the wrong place?

digging in the wrong place is **stinkier** than moldy cheese. I think we should go find Professor Mouserson."

They all agreed **immediately**.

"But how will we get there?" Colette asked.

Nicky **winked** and shot her friends a **sly** look. "Since we're in Egypt, let's travel like the pharaohs did — on the **Nile**."

EVERYONE
TO THE DIG!

A few hours later, the five mouselets were sailing down the Nile River. The **WATER** was an intense blue, with small silvery **WAVES**. The wind filled the sails of the felucca* the Thea Sisters had rented. The breeze that ruffled the mouselets' fur was a welcome relief from the **BURNING** sun.

Pam gave Nicky a pat on the tail. "Great idea, Nick! This boat is **AMAZING**!"

As they made their way south, the green of the sugar **cane** and the white, yellow, and pink of the acacia **flowers** gave way to the intense gold of the **desert** sands.

Paulina tried once again to phone the

---

* A *felucca* is a small sailboat with a long, narrow hull.

professor, but with no luck. "Uh-oh. My cell battery is dead!"

"When we get to the dig, they're sure to have **NEWS** about Professor Sparkle," Violet reassured her.

"And Professor Mouserson will be there," Nicky added. "If he doesn't know where Professor Sparkle is, at least he'll be able to help us **LOOK** for him."

As the felucca approached the riverbank, the boatmouse interrupted them. "The camp is over there!" he said, **pointing** at a hill.

"We're here?" Paulina asked **hopefully**.

The boatmouse **SMiLED** and pointed to a rodent seated on the riverbank. "No! He'll take you over the hill."

Violet wrinkled her forehead, **PERPLEXED**. "Is he a taxi driver?"

Nicky burst out **laughing**. "Yep, he's

definitely a taxi driver!" she exclaimed. Then she pointed at the camels tied up nearby. "Except *those* are his **TAXIS**!"

This was the first time the Thea Sisters had **TRAVELED** on the backs of camels, and most of them were nervous, especially Colette. For Nicky, who'd spent half her life on horseback, it was no big deal.

"Whoa!" Colette **grumbled**. "This ride is bumpier than **Blue cheese**! I hope I don't get motion sickness."

"Mouselets, there's only one way out of this **HEAT**," Paulina pointed out. "And it's better to go on the back of a **camel** than by paw."

So they set off. After a few minutes, even Colette had gotten used to the swaying motion of the animal.

When they reached the dig, the sun was **setting**. From the top of the hill, the Thea Sisters could see the Nile flowing gently behind them. It was red and gold from the sun's **reflection**. The **Ruins** were bathed in soft yellow light.

The **archaeologists** and the workers they'd hired must have just stopped working. The former were returning to their tents, and

the latter were making the trip back to their villages.

One of the archaeologists noticed that the little caravan of camels had arrived, and **scurried** over to meet them. It was Dunya, Professor Sparkle's colleague — the one they'd seen in the **PHOTOGRAPH**.

A wide smile stretched across Dunya's snout as she reached out a paw and helped Violet get down from her camel. "You've finally arrived! We were expecting you." Then she **LOOKED** around and added, "But where's Bart?"

Dunya

PROFESSOR SPARKLE'S DISAPPEARANCE

It quickly became clear that no one knew where **Professor Sparkle** had gone. Professor Mouserson seemed irritated when he heard the **news** about his disappearance, but he didn't seem very worried. "That young rodent is a big know-it-all! He's got a snout full of strange ideas, but I don't think he knows his Muenster from his mozzarella. It wouldn't surprise me if he had decided to go **dig** somewhere else."

Professor Marcus Mouserson

His colleagues seemed to agree with him. Or maybe they didn't **dare** contradict him. Professor Mouserson had a very strict and **BOSSY** way about him!

"There's no reason to worry," Professor Mouserson declared. "You'll see. Your **professor** will spend a few days digging some useless hole in the sand, and then he'll return with his tail between his paws."

The Thea Sisters were **OUTRAGED** by Mouserson's lack of concern for their teacher. Nicky was so upset, it was all Colette, Pamela, Paulina, and Violet could do to restrain her.

Luckily, Dunya was there. Though she was Professor Mouserson's assistant, she was definitely worried. "Are you sure that Bart didn't leave anything behind?" she asked the mouselets **nervously**. "Not even a note?"

"Nothing," said Paulina, shaking her snout.

Dunya looked **discouraged**. But she accompanied the Thea Sisters to the **TENT** that had been prepared for them.

"Don't pay attention to that **ornery** old rodent!" she whispered to them. "Bart told me his new theory about the **TREASURE OF THE SUN**'s location. I think it's brilliant, even though Professor Mouserson thinks Bart is just an amateur!"

"As a matter of fact, we think he might be on the **RIGHT** track," Paulina said.

"The professor told us that according to his calculations, the Treasure of the Sun is buried someplace else," Violet added.

Dunya stared at her intently, a **WARY** look on her snout. "Your professor must have a lot of faith in you. . . ."

The Thea Sisters **blushed** with pride.

"Look, Bart and Professor Mouserson had a terrible **FIGHT**," Dunya continued. "I started arguing with Mouserson myself. He ended up kicking Bart out of the **dig**."

"Really?" Pam exclaimed.

The Thea Sisters looked at one another.

They couldn't believe what they'd heard!

Nicky squeaked for all of them. "We don't understand. Professor Sparkle seems to have DISAPPEARED! Even if they fought, how can Professor Mouserson be so unconcerned? What could have happened to Professor Sparkle?"

Dunya smiled. "You're right to be worried, mouselets. I need to explain a few things. But you must promise to tell me EVERYTHING that Bart said and did before he disappeared!"

Professors Mouserson and Sparkle had an argument before the Thea Sisters arrived. Could their fight have something to do with the professor's disappearance?

PROFESSOR SPARKLE'S THEORY

Dunya and the Thea Sisters made themselves comfortable inside the **TENT**.

"As I'm sure you already know, Professor Mouserson found an old papyrus with **instructions** for finding the Treasure of the Sun," the young archaeologist explained. "He's convinced that the place described is right here, where we are now."

"Right," Colette said. "But then why does **Professor Sparkle** think that Professor Mouserson is wrong?"

"It's because the text on the papyrus isn't clear at all," Dunya explained. "It's full of phrases that are **poetic** and difficult to understand. For example, *'The scarab god, Khepri, brought to light the Treasure of Ra, hidden from Atum-Ra, passing through the narrow belt that leads to Sopdet.'*

"Huh?!" Pam exclaimed, **wrinkling** her forehead. Then she started to think it through. "So Khepri is the **scarab**, Ra is the sun, and Atum-Ra is also the sun, but at sunset. So who's this Sopdet dude?"

Pam's **saucy** style of squeaking made Dunya giggle. "HA-HA! Sopdet is the Egyptian name for the star Sirius," she

THE STAR SIRIUS

Sirius, the Dog Star, was a very important star for the ancient Egyptians. **Sopdet** was the goddess associated with this star. Each year, Sopdet would appear at dawn at the beginning of the flood season.

replied. "Professor Mouserson found a **lapis lazuli** scarab at the beginning of the excavation. It was similar to the statue in Karnak, and that convinced Mouserson that he'd found the **right** spot!"

"*The scarab god, Khepri, brought to light the Treasure of Ra*'!" Violet repeated. "That's what it said on the **papyrus**. So Professor Mouserson thinks the Treasure of the Sun is here because the scarab was here."

Dunya nodded. "Exactly! Except we've been digging here for months and nothing significant has **emerged** — nothing that's connected to the Treasure of the Sun."

"So that's why Professor Sparkle came up with his own theory," Nicky said.

"Yes. Bart thought that perhaps the scarab Mouserson found was just another clue, which would **lead** to another place. . . ."

Dunya looked discouraged. "Oh, I can't explain this without a map!"

"No problem!" Paulina chimed in. She pulled her trusty paw-held computer out of her backpack. "We'll use the Internet!"

Paulina made a few quick keystrokes, and a detailed map of the archaeological site

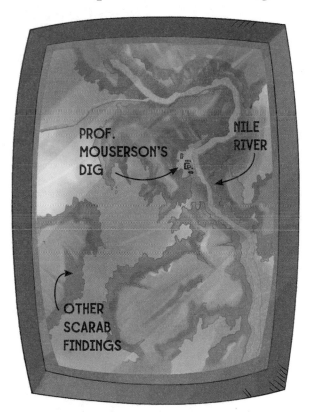

appeared **on-screen**.

Dunya pointed to a **spot** on the map. "This area is vast and **DANGEROUS**, so it hasn't been explored much. But other statues of **scarabs** have been found there — similar to the one Professor Mouserson found. According to Bart, if you interpret their positions, you can trace the exact location of the Treasure of the Sun."

Violet nodded in **excitement**. "The professor could be right! Many Egyptian artifacts hide secrets. But why would Professor Mouserson ignore this possibility?"

Dunya **sighed**. "It took Mouserson years to find this place. He doesn't want to admit that he's made a mistake!"

The **mouselets** nodded. Finally, the situation was a bit clearer.

ORION'S BELT

After their long trip and intense DISCUSSION with Dunya, the Thea Sisters were exhausted. They decided to call it a night. They settled down to rest in their tent.

The night was calm and the sky was full of stars. Not a creature was stirring, not even another mouse.

Despite this, none of the mouselets were able to fall asleep. They couldn't stop thinking about their teacher's DISAPPEARANCE. It made no sense!

Colette got up from her cot and started to scurry back and forth. "Mouselets, I'm so nervous I think I need to wash my fur!" She rummaged around in her backpack for her shampoo. "Moldy mozzarella!" she grumbled. "Where could it be? I know I packed it. . . . Wait, what's this? Oh my goodmouse, it's Professor Sparkle's bag!"

Nicky **JUMPED** up from her cot. "Holey cheese!"

Colette suddenly remembered. "Of course! The professor asked me to hold his bag for him back in Karnak. Once we were back at the hotel, I put it here in my bag, and then I **forgot** all about it!"

Now all five mouselets were on their paws, crowding around the professor's bag.

"**Open it!**" Pam encouraged her. "I'll bet you there's a clue inside!"

Colette looked at the others **doubtfully**. "It's not nice to snoop around in other people's things."

But everyone agreed with Pam: This was an **emergency**! So Colette undid the zipper and peeked inside. "There are some papers, pens, some coins, and . . . a **NOTEBOOK**!"

Paulina grabbed it. "It's the notebook the professor used to write down the scarab's measurements." She started to **FLIP** through it. "It's filled with notes — look! There are sketches, too."

CLUE!

Violet pointed to one. "**Hey**, I recognize this one! It's the constellation Orion."

Then she read Professor Sparkle's note, which included an ARROW pointing to the drawing. "'*When the locations of the scarab statues are connected on a map, they form the constellation Orion'*!"

"**Cheese niblets**!" Pam exclaimed.

"And the star Sirius, or Sopdet, is part of

All of Professor Sparkle's discoveries are written down in his notebook. Would the professor have gone in search of the Treasure of the Sun without it?

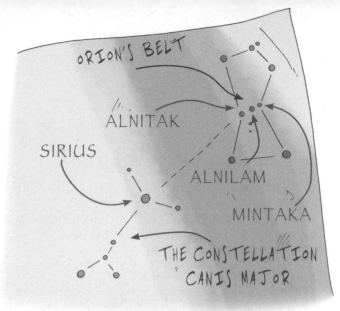

Orion, right?" Colette guessed.

"No, but it's close by," said Paulina, showing the others the **DRawiNg** in the notebook. "These three stars are called Orion's belt. If you trace down, you'll find the star Sirius — part of the constellation Canis Major. . . ."

"*The scarab god, Khepri, brought to light the Treasure of Ra, hidden from Atum-Ra, passing through the narrow belt that leads to Sopdet,*'" Violet recited. "That's what's on the papyrus."

Paulina picked up her computer. "So that's

THE CONSTELLATION ORION

Orion (also called the Hunter) is one of the brightest constellations that has been seen since ancient times. Close to Orion is the constellation Canis Major, whose brightest star is Sirius.

ARCHITECTURE AND CONSTELLATIONS

Some modern scientists believe that the pyramids were designed to line up with the stars. For example, according to some Egyptologists, the alignment of the three important pyramids Khufu, Khafre, and Menkaure corresponds perfectly with the alignment of the three stars in Orion's belt.

Menkaure — MINTAKA

Khafre

ALNILAM

Khufu — ALNITAK

the reason for all those measurements!"

The friends HUDDLED around her.

"What do you mean?" Pamela asked, CURIOUS.

"Just wait one second," Paulina mumbled, her paws flying over the tiny keyboard.

"I'm confirming the professor's theory. I'm taking the star map of the **constellation** Orion and lining it up with the points where scarabs have been found. And there we have it: *They match!*"

She marked a line on the screen that linked all the scarabs. They matched the three stars in Orion's belt! Next Paulina extended the line all the way to the star Sirius. Then she looked at the point that corresponded

TAP
TAP
TAP

with Sirius on the **map**.

"They point to the area where the other scarabs have been found!" Nicky exclaimed. "That must be where the treasure of the sun is buried!"

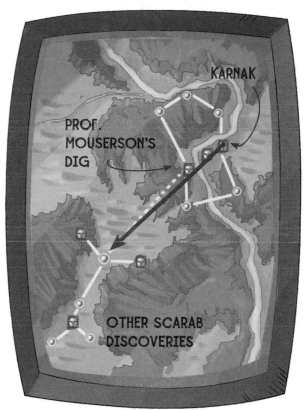

KARNAK

PROF. MOUSERSON'S DIG

OTHER SCARAB DISCOVERIES

NIGHT OF SHADOWS

Now none of the Thea Sisters could even think about sleep. They had only one thing on their minds: **REACHING** the area Paulina had pinpointed on the map.

"Mouselets, there's only one rodent who can help us now: Professor Mouserson," Violet admitted in **despair**. "He's got everything in this camp under his paw."

Pam **shook** her snout. "Professor Mouserson will never help us! He's already made clear what he thinks of Professor Sparkle."

"Yes, but what if the professor is in **DANGER**?" Nicky replied. "Something must have happened to him!"

Paulina nodded. "Nicky's right. We need to convince Professor Mouserson of that, and then we need to get an **SUV** so we can go find Professor Sparkle. . . ."

"And we need to do it *soon*!" Pam added.

Colette shivered. "What do you mean, 'soon'?! It's the middle of the night! And it's colder than iced cheese. **Brrr** . . ."

"It doesn't matter," Nicky replied. "We don't have a minute to lose!"

The mouselets **QUICKLY** got dressed and slipped out of their tent, quiet as mice.

The Thea Sisters crossed the campsite silently. Pamela noticed a faint **light** coming from one of the tents.

"That must be Professor Mouserson's tent," she whispered.

But just at that moment, a shadowy figure **POPPED** out from another **tent**. It was Dunya!

Dunya almost jumped out of her fur when

she saw the five **SHADOWS**. The Thea Sisters realized she was coming from **Professor Sparkle**'s tent.

"I was **anxious** about Bart!" Dunya explained once she was sure that they were safe from prying eyes and ears. "I thought I might find a **CLUE** in his tent."

"Did you **FIND** anything?" Paulina asked.

Dunya **shook** her snout. "Nothing, unfortunately."

Colette pulled out Professor Sparkle's notebook with a **flourish**. "But we found something!"

Dunya's **EYES** lit up, and she immediately put out her paw to take the notebook. "His **notes**!"

But Colette held on tightly. "The professor **TRUSTED** me with this!" she explained. "I have to protect it for him."

Why is Dunya sneaking around in the middle of the night?

The professor trusted me with this!

CLUE!

"Oh, yes, of course, I understand," Dunya muttered. She looked disappointed.

"We think **Professor Sparkle** must have gone to the area southwest of the Nile," Paulina explained.

"We want to go look for him, and to do that we need an **SUV**!" said Pam.

Dunya seemed enthusiastic about the idea. "Trust me, **mouselets**! I'll take care of everything. And I'm coming with you!"

Why is Dunya so eager to read Professor Sparkle's notebook?

A RESCUE MISSION

First thing the next morning, the little group began preparing for their desert rescue mission. By the time they were ready to leave **CAMP**, it was already well into the afternoon.

Dunya had managed to **WRANGLE** permission from Professor Mouserson to go in search of "that **ARROGANT** young rodent," as he called him. Professor Mouserson had agreed to provide the little group with a vehicle and enough food and **water** to last three days.

The trip wouldn't be too long, but the ride through the dunes was bumpy. At the lowest points of this wild area, the **SUV** had to go slowly to keep from flipping over. **Luckily**, Dunya was a confident driver. Almost too confident, actually . . .

CLUE!

"Dunya seems to know this area well," Paulina WHiSPeReD to Violet, who was sitting next to her.

Her friend nodded **thoughtfully**. "True. There aren't any road signs, but she hasn't stopped once to look at the map. . . ."

The sun was just beginning to **set**, but when they made their way into a narrow opening between the cliffs, it felt like it was already **NIGHTTIME**. They were heading through an enormouse, pitch-black canyon.

Nicky spoke up. "Maybe we should **STOP**, Dunya. It's darker than the inside of a cat's mouth in here."

"And bumpier than a cat's tongue!" said Violet as they bounced over a pothole.

"It's too **DANGEROUS**!" Colette agreed. "Slow down so we don't **break** our tails!"

But Dunya didn't listen to the Thea Sisters'

It's strange that Dunya knows this area so well. It's almost as if she's been down this road before. . . .

warnings. "Hold **TIGHT** to your fur, mouselets! I'm looking for a good place to spend the night."

"But if you go the wrong way, we'll get stuck!" cried Pam. Pam was a good driver herself, and she didn't understand how Dunya could be so confident on such **HAZARDOUS** roads. But the archaeologist didn't seem to hear her.

After another half hour of **JUMPS** and bumps, the walls of the canyon finally opened up, and the land became flat.

"A fire!" Paulina shouted, pointing into the distance. "Up ahead! Do you **SEE** that?"

"There are **lights**, too! It must be a camp!" Nicky said.

Dunya said nothing, but she slowed down and honked the **HORN** several times.

BEE-BEE-BEEEP! BEE-BEE-BEEEP!

Several **SHADOWS** drew close to them. "Professor Sparkle!" Colette squealed. She'd recognized their teacher. Four **LARGE** rodents surrounded him.

WHAT DO YOU MAKE OF THE SITUATION SO FAR?

1) Professor Sparkle mysteriously disappeared from Karnak, and since then he hasn't answered his phone.

2) His theory about the Treasure of the Sun upset the famouse Professor Mouserson.

3) The only other mouse who's worried about Professor Sparkle is Dunya. But even she is acting strangely.

4) The Thea Sisters found the professor's notebook, which contains important notes about the location of the Treasure of the Sun. Dunya is very interested in this notebook.

5) The Thea Sisters and Dunya took an SUV to look for Professor Sparkle. Dunya seems to know exactly where she's going, as if she's gone this way before.

THIEVES AND JACKALS

The Thea Sisters jumped out of the SUV and **scurried** to meet their professor. They were overjoyed to find him safe and sound. They all started squeaking at once.

"What are you doing here, Professor?"

"Why did you DISAPPEAR without telling us where you were going?"

"Have you found the Treasure of the Sun?"

To the Thea Sisters' *surprise*, the professor looked deeply worried. He wasn't at all *happy* to see them!

The professor looked Dunya right in the eye. His snout was red — he was **angry**!

"You shouldn't have brought them here!" he shouted. "It won't do any good. You can't take them prisoner, too!"

Violet, Nicky, Paulina, and Colette stared at the professor, their snouts hanging open.

PRISONER???

Pamela burst out laughing. "Ha ha ha! Are you joking, Professor? Is this really the time to twist our tails?"

But her laughter was cut short when the **MOUSELETS** noticed the icy glare Dunya was giving their professor. She had a **WICKED** sneer on her snout.

"You and your students left me no choice, Bart!" Dunya snapped. "This fresh French mouselet would **NEVER** paw over your precious notebook. But now you don't have any more excuses for delaying the **dig**. It's time to find the treasure!"

The Thea Sisters jumped. Dunya's harsh tone made their whiskers quiver!

Professor Sparkle's expression grew even **DARKER**. "Let them go at once, or I won't help you at all!"

At that moment, the **burliest** of the four rodents grabbed him by the collar and **LIFTED** him off the ground.

"Shut your snout, or you'll be sorry!"

"Put him **DOWN**, Tim!" Dunya ordered. Then she turned back to Professor Sparkle. This time, she used her sweetest, most

persuasive squeak. "I am the only one who believes in your theory, Bart. We wouldn't be here otherwise, don't you see?"

Then she smiled, but so **SHARPLY** that it sent a chill down Paulina's tail. It was unbelievable: Dunya seemed like a completely different rodent!

"For years, I've followed that **old BLABBERMOUSE** Mouserson!" she continued. "And what has it gotten me? *Nothing!* It seemed like he was so close to finding the Treasure of the Sun, but there's nothing where he's digging but **junk**!"

Professor Sparkle burst out, "You're wrong! Mouserson is a **true** Egyptologist, while you and your henchmice are nothing but thieves and jackals! You're just searching for **gold**, not knowledge. I should have realized that right away!"

"**Hee hee hee!**" Dunya sneered. Her creepy cackle echoed through the campsite. "*Just* gold, did you say?" she replied. "Oh no, my dear professor! Jewelry, too! **Precious** stones! The greatest treasure of all time!"

The Thea Sisters couldn't believe it. They had trusted Dunya, and they'd been **fooled**! Now they understood Dunya's interest in the professor's notebook.

Dunya returned to the **SUV**, rummaged around in their bags, and placed three objects on the hood: Professor Sparkle's **notebook**, a papyrus scroll, and a scarab made of lapis lazuli that was as large as her paw.

"You **STOLE** the papyrus and the scarab from Mouserson!" Professor Sparkle exclaimed.

Dunya just **smiled**. "This valuable scarab may serve us well even before we sell it." She turned to the Thea Sisters. "You five are going to help us find the treasure, or you and your precious professor just might get lost in the desert. Do you understand me?"

The mouselets looked at one another. Then they turned to Professor Sparkle. He clenched his paws.

Tim saw it. He **clenched** his paws, too, and smirked toward the mouselets.

Professor Sparkle stepped forward. "We'll all cooperate. Right, mouselets?"

The Thea Sisters nodded reluctantly. What other choice did they have? They were Dunya's 𝕡𝕣𝕚𝕤𝕠𝕟𝕖𝕣𝕤!

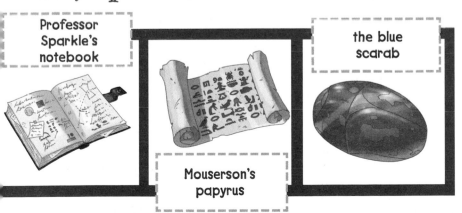

Professor Sparkle's notebook

Mouserson's papyrus

the blue scarab

DIG!

The next day, everyone got ready to dig. The **measurements** Professor Sparkle had jotted in his notebook would make it possible to find the location of the pharaoh's temple, and Dunya wanted to get started right away.

"What should we do?" Nicky asked her friends as soon as they had a moment alone.

"I don't think we have much choice," Paulina replied.

Pam agreed. "We have to **HELP** Professor Sparkle."

The mouselets showed Dunya the two **maps** Paulina had superimposed, one on top of the other — one of the landscape and one of the constellation Orion.

Dunya examined the two maps, which also

gave the exact positions of the statues of the scarab god, Khepri. She traced a LiNe from each of them and . . .

"The lines all lead to a single point in an open area," **Violet** observed reluctantly.

Dunya snickered. "Elementary, my dear mouse! And that's where we must **dig**!"

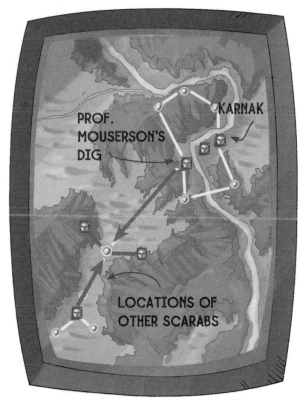

PROF. MOUSERSON'S DIG

KARNAK

LOCATIONS OF OTHER SCARABS

The spot wasn't very far away. After a journey of just a few hours, the excavation began at a **FRENZIED** pace. It went on day and night.

The mouselets were determined to look for a way to **escape**, but it was difficult. Dunya's henchmice watched over them like they were the last morsels of cheese on earth!

As the days passed, fragments of columns, **shattered** statues, and slabs of **STONE** began to emerge from beneath the **sand**. But it wasn't until Pamela found a huge pink granite carving that they were sure that the Treasure of the Sun was nearby.

"Another scarab!" Pam exclaimed.

Dunya studied the angle of the statue and ordered them to focus their **excavation** in the direction the scarab's head was pointing. She had learned a lot from **Professor Sparkle**.

After another hour of intense work, the soil collapsed into a hole so deep they couldn't see its bottom.

"**Stop!**" Dunya cried. "We need to rest before we try going underground."

The Thea Sisters collapsed, **exhausted**, under a tent. So did Professor Sparkle and Dunya's thugs. It was hotter than a fondue pot!

The only one who didn't rest was Dunya. She was curled up in her tent, studying Professor Mouserson's **papyrus**.

"*'Only the wisdom of the scarab god, Khepri, will lead to the Treasure of the Sun'!*" she muttered. "It won't be easy to reach the treasure. The Egyptians often made it difficult to access their treasures in order to protect them!"

"I don't like this, Dunya," Tim **muttered**. "I don't want to be buried alive down in some rat hole just because we haven't solved an ancient **riddle**."

Dunya patted him on the tail and **CACKLED**. "No worries, Tim. Bart will be the one to risk his **FUR**, not us!"

DEEP UNDERGROUND

It wasn't quite dawn the next morning when Dunya woke Professor Sparkle and told him what she wanted him to do.

"**NO, NO, ABSOLUTELY NOT!**" the professor shouted in reply. "I'm not going to help you with this **ROBBERY**!"

The professor's angry squeaks woke up the Thea Sisters all the way in the next tent. They scurried over to see what was going on.

"What's happening?" Paulina asked.

The professor was **furious**. "Dunya wants me to go after the treasure! She won't risk her own fur, so she's sending me instead!"

Violet turned to Dunya and crossed her paws. "A rodent can't **go down** there all alone! It's too **DANGEROUS**!"

"Afraid you'll lose your dear professor? Well, why don't you go down there with him!" Dunya replied **DEFIANTLY**.

But if Dunya thought she could frighten the Thea Sisters, she was **SORELY** mistaken.

"Great idea! We'll all go," Nicky replied.

"No, not the **mouselets**!" Professor Sparkle interrupted, alarmed. "I'll go!"

"**Hee hee hee!** You're *pathetic*!" Dunya

We'll go underground with the professor!

said. "Very well: All six of you will go down to find the treasure for me."

Dunya didn't waste any time. She pawed them all **ROPES**, flashlights, helmets, and other necessary instruments for their **task**. Then she attached a microcamera to Professor Sparkle's helmet so she could watch them.

"I'll see everything on my computer **screen**. It'll be like I'm right there next to you," she warned them. "So no **TRICKS**!"

Finally, Dunya gave the little group the papyrus and the lapis lazuli scarab. "These should be useful to you. Now it's time to get going. Move those tails!"

Professor Sparkle was the first to be **LOWERED** into the hole. When he reached the bottom, he called for the mouselets to join him, but to be careful.

The shaft dropped into a small underground chamber with a tunnel leading out of it. Nicky **shivered** at the thought of squeezing through there. When she had **COURAGEOUSLY** offered to follow the professor, she hadn't been thinking about her claustrophobia. Nicky hated being in small, closed-up places.

Violet squeezed her paw. "Come on, Nicky! Don't be a 'fraidy mouse. Take a deep breath. We're all here with you!"

Nicky smiled and nodded. She took a deep breath and went forward.

The tunnel was **twisty** and narrow. Suddenly, they arrived in a larger second room with three doorways.

"Which path do we take, Professor?" Pam asked.

While he consulted the papyrus, the

mouselets **LOOKED** around.

"There are hieroglyphs on the doorframes!" Paulina noticed. "What do they mean?"

"'*Akhet*' . . . '*Peret*' . . . '*Shomu*' . . . ," Professor Sparkle read aloud, puzzled.

THE EGYPTIAN CALENDAR

The Egyptians based their calendar on the periodic rise and fall of the Nile. The year was divided into three seasons, each one lasting four months.

THE SEASONS

The first season was called **Akhet**, which means "flood." In this season, which lasted from July through October, the Nile flooded its banks.

Next came **Peret**, or "the withdrawal," which lasted from November through February. During **Peret**, the Nile receded, so it was possible to plant crops.

Finally came **Shomu**, or "dryness," which lasted from March through June. This was the period for harvesting grain, when the Nile waters reached their lowest level.

In THE LABYRINTH

The Thea Sisters and Professor Sparkle didn't know which path to take.

"Professor, does the papyrus give any hints?" Paulina asked.

Professor Sparkle **scanned** the ancient paper again. "Here it says, *'The path of the scarab god, Khepri, is dark but follows the powerful Ra.'*"

"Ra is the god of the SUN during the day," said Pamela, thinking aloud.

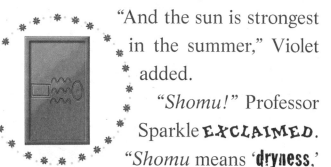

"And the sun is strongest in the summer," Violet added.

"*Shomu!*" Professor Sparkle EXCLAIMED. "*Shomu* means '**dryness**,' because it's the hottest part of the year! The season in which Ra — that is, the sun — is most **powerful**!"

So the mouselets and their professor went through the doorway marked with the hieroglyph *Shomu*. The corridor descended farther into the bowels of the **EARTH**.

Meanwhile, Dunya followed their progress step-by-step, thanks to the **camera** on Professor Sparkle's helmet. But she had made one mistake: She hadn't attached a microphone, so she couldn't understand why the mice chose one route over another.

When the corridor finally ended, they found themselves in a

Why did they choose that path?!

new chamber. For a moment, they were **AFRAID** that they had ended up back where they'd started, but then they saw that this room had four doorways, not three. And there were ʃimple decorations on the walls, but no hieroglyphs!

"Four doorways, like the four months that made up each season for the Egyptians!" Violet said. She focused on the doorframes. "But there's nothing written here. . . ."

The other mouselets were examining the walls carefully, looking for clues, when all of a sudden . . .

"EEEEEEEEEEEEEEEK!"

Pamela's scream made them all jump.

"What is it?! Did you see something?" Professor Sparkle spluttered, terrified.

Pam pointed at the floor and stuttered, "There — a B-B-B-BUG!"

Paulina bent over, brushed the sand with her paw, and shined her flashlight on a small scarab — made of black stone.

Colette giggled nervously. "You're really stuck on scarabs, Pam!"

"Don't laugh! This one looked real," Pamela grumbled.

Until then, the ground had been made of solid earth. But this room had a tiled floor that was covered with a thin layer of sand. When they brushed off the tiles, the mouselets and the professor discovered four scarabs, each pointing to a different doorway.

Nicky rummaged through the TOOLS and found a chisel. She used it to chip around one of the scarabs. In just a few minutes, she'd popped it out. When she turned it over, she found a hieroglyph on the bottom.

"*Payni!* That's the name of the second

month in the season *Shomu,*" Professor Sparkle explained.

Paulina plucked out the second scarab, Colette the third, and Violet the fourth. Each one was marked with the name of a month.

"CLEARLY we need to choose one. But which one?" Paulina wondered.

"*Mesore!*" Professor Sparkle exclaimed with **determination**. "We must take the

Mesore corridor. *Mesore* means 'birth of Ra' . . . the birth of the sun!"

Violet's **snout** lit up. "I read about that in one of your course books, Professor! The birth of the sun comes at dawn. And according to the Egyptians, when the sun rises on the **horizon**, it shines like the Treasure of the Sun!"

"That's **correct**!" Professor Sparkle exclaimed. "That must be the **RIGHT** direction."

The Thea Sisters hurried to put the scarabs back. Then they followed the **professor** through the doorway and down a long corridor that went up and down and up again, twisting and turning, until . . .

"Oh, no! It's **blocked**!" cried Colette.

THE WISDOM
OF THE SCARAB

"Bart, you **complete cheddarface**!" Dunya screamed. "You took the wrong path!"

Since the mouselets and Professor Sparkle had gone **UNDERGROUND**, Dunya's eyes had been glued to the **computer** screen. Using her camera's perch on top of

Professor **Sparkle**'s helmet, she had followed their every move. She was itching to get her paws on the treasure.

Back in the tunnel, Professor Sparkle looked sadly at the enormouse **BOULDER** that blocked the end of the hallway.

"Uh-oh," he **mumbled**. "I guess we'll have to turn back."

The mouselets and Professor Sparkle did an **about-snout** and started to move back through the tunnel.

"There are only four hallways. Sooner or later we'll find the right one," Nicky said, trying to cheer everyone up.

Only Violet remained in front of the boulder. She had a **pensive** look.

Colette turned around and called back to her, "Aren't you coming, Vi?"

"'*The* Scarabaeus sacer *stores nourishment*

and eggs in balls larger than itself, then **rolls** *them on the ground all the way to its nest,'"* Violet muttered.

Colette said, confused, "Is that one of Grandpa Chen's 𝒞𝒽𝒾𝓃𝑒𝓈𝑒 proverbs?"

"No! I read it in the footnotes of that book Professor Sparkle assigned," Violet explained. Without **LOOKING** away from the boulder, she added, "Maybe we should **PUSH** this boulder as a scarab would and make it roll away!"

SCARABAEUS SACER

The *Scarabaeus sacer,* or "sacred scarab," is very common in Egypt, and the ancient Egyptians believed it was holy. The scarab deposits its eggs in small balls of fresh dung and then rolls them to safety. Ancient Egyptians believed that a giant scarab formed the sun this way and then rolled it over the horizon and across the sky each day.

"Did I hear you right? You want to move that **MASSIVE** boulder?!" Pam exclaimed.

"The papyrus says, '*Only the wisdom of the scarab god, Khepri, will allow you to reach the Treasure of the Sun*'!" Violet persisted. "If you ask me, that means that we need to think and act like scarabs!"

Pam crossed her paws. "Do what you like, **mouselets**, but I *refuse* to get inside the head of one of those creatures!"

She looked so **funny** with a scowl on her usually cheerful snout that everyone burst out laughing. "**Ha ha ha!**"

A good laugh was exactly what they needed to calm their jangled nerves.

Back at the camp, Dunya and Tim watched their prisoners in confusion. *What would make these six cheeseheads laugh at a time like this?!* Dunya thought. She didn't

understand the value of a laugh among friends.

Professor Sparkle thought about what Violet had said. He had to admit that her idea made sense. "I think Violet might be onto something. I know it seems like an impossible task, but let's see if we can **PUSH** this boulder away."

"You're the boss, **PROFESSOR**!" Pamela declared. She rolled up her sleeves. "Now you'll see Super Pam in action!"

While Colette, Violet, and Paulina **shined**

their flashlights, Professor Sparkle, Pam, and Nicky leaned against the boulder. On the count of "**ONE, TWO, THREE . . . PUSH!**" they started to push with all their **MIGHT**.

At first, nothing happened.

"Rat-munching rattlesnakes, this thing is **HEAVY**!" Nicky muttered.

But little by little, unbelievably . . . the boulder started to **roll**!

"We're doing it!" Pam rejoiced.

After the first push, the enormouse rock moved with surprising **ease**.

"Hey . . . *puff puff* . . . this tunnel is going downhill!" cried Professor Sparkle. His snout was red from effort. "That's why we're able to **MOVE** the boulder!"

In fact, the boulder seemed to be on a gently sloping chute. It started to roll along slowly.

A SENSATIONAL DISCOVERY!

At the end of the chute, the **BOULDER** came to a rest, and the Thea Sisters and the professor fell to the ground, exhausted.

"OOF!"

They were now at the end of the corridor. They looked around and realized they'd reached a large **SEMICIRCULAR** balcony overlooking an enormouse empty room.

Nicky **REACTED** first. She *HURRIED* to the edge of the balcony to get a better look.

Right in front of her was a deep pit. Beyond the pit was a huge doorway made of rock, but it was too far away to reach by *JUMPING*. Darkness made it impossible to see what lay beyond it.

"Oh, no! Our **flashlight** batteries are almost dead, mouselets!" Paulina said.

"Don't **worry**!" Professor Sparkle said. "I have **TORCHES** with me. One of the first things you learn on a dig is never to risk losing light when you're underground."

Each rodent lit a large torch and joined Nicky at the **EDGE** of the pit. The torches illuminated the space below them. A glimmer of gold reflected in front of them.

"**THE TREASURE OF THE SUN!**" all six exclaimed together. Their jaws **dropped** in **amazement**.

"Just look at it, mouselets!" Pam sighed. "It's shinier than a sweaty slice of Swiss."

They'd finally found the ancient **TREASURE**! It was there ahead of them. They could almost see it, but it was impossible to reach it over the deep pit.

"We . . . we can't go on, mouselets," Professor Sparkle announced, his squeak cracking with **emotion**. "We'll have to return to the surface and build a bridge."

They turned around, and suddenly an incredible **sight** appeared before them. They hadn't realized that the wall behind the balcony was decorated with a **dazzling** mural! The **PAINTING** showed the

banks of the Nile River, covered with plants, **FL✿wers**, multicolored birds, and even a crocodile.

"**How gorgeous**," breathed Colette as she and the other mouselets drew nearer.

"This mural is **perfectly** preserved," Professor Sparkle added, his eyes shining. "What a **fabumouse** discovery!"

FOLLOWING DIRECTIONS

For a few minutes, the **extraordinary** beauty of the paintings distracted the group from the Treasure of the Sun.

"Hey! There are **HOLES** in the wall!" Nicky noticed.

In fact, on the far left section of the wall, there were five oval-shaped openings: four small ones, and one **LARGER** one in the middle. Each hole was evenly shaped.

Colette **wrinkled** her snout in concentration. "**HMM!** These holes remind me of something. . . ." Then, without squeaking any

further, she turned around and scurried down the corridor.

"What are you doing, Coco?" her friends shouted.

Her response was FAINT: "I need to go get something. . . ."

Meanwhile, back at the camp, Dunya was shaking with **IMPATIENCE**.

"Grrr! What are those DUNCES doing now?! Why aren't they looking for a way to **reach** the treasure? They're almost there!"

Tim tried to reason with her. "There's a giant pit! What can they do?"

But Dunya was

GRRR!!!

stubborn. "There's a way, I'm sure of it! They just need to get their **cheese brains** to work!"

In the meantime, Colette had returned **TRIUMPHANTLY**. She was carrying the four scarabs they'd removed from the floor. Her friends crowded around her, **curious**.

"I'm not the best at **PUZZLES**, but I think this might work like jewels set in a necklace," Colette explained as she placed one of the scarabs in each of the small holes in the wall.

"*Et voilà!*" she exclaimed with **SATISFACTION**. "It's like they were made to fit these holes!"

"They *were* made to fit these holes!" Violet agreed. "It can't be a coincidence!"

Paulina *clapped* her paws with glee. "You go, gerbil!"

The four scarabs fit perfectly into the four smaller holes in the wall. Only the center hole remained **EMPTY**.

"What about this one? What's supposed to go there?" Pam asked as she pointed to the hole.

"How about the **lapis lazuli scarab**?" Nicky suggested.

Sparkle smacked his snout.

SMACK!

"Of course! I forgot we had it!"

"Before we put it in, let's **read** what's written on the bottom," Violet suggested.

The professor read aloud, "'**The treasure of the Sun passes through the dark waters of Atum-Ra, but Khepri will turn the great wheel and raise it up to the sky.**'"

Colette smiled. "That's very poetic, don't you think?"

"I guess so," Pam commented. "But, mouselets, all this poetry and metaphors and stuff . . . that's just not how I roll. Why couldn't the ancient Egyptians just leave us SiMPLe directions to follow?"

Nicky grinned. "I'm with you, Pam!"

The professor held the scarab up against

the wall. "It looks like it's the right size. . . ."
He had to push **HARD** to fit the scarab
into the hole, but when he succeeded, they
heard a mighty rumbling noise.

CRRRRRREEEEAAAAAK

Everything around them began to shake.
The mouselets grabbed one another's paws
and held on tight. Then something broke
loose from the floor right in front of their
ASTONISHED eyes. . . .

A huge stone wheel was **RISING** from
the ground!

"**JUMPING** tuna fish!" Nicky cried.
"What is it?"

THE MYSTERIOUS WHEEL

As soon as the floor stopped shaking, the Thea Sisters and Professor Sparkle **nervously** approached the strange, enormouse **WHEEL**. What could it possibly be used for?

"It looks like the helm of a **SHIP** . . . ," Pam guessed. "But on its side."

"It reminds me of the **merry-go-round** that my little sister, Maria, and I used to play on!" Paulina sighed. Her eyes clouded over with **SADNESS**. "I haven't been able to call Maria since we left Mouserson's camp. She must think I've forgotten about her. . . ."

"Maybe it really is a **merry-go-round**," Violet suggested. "And we have to make it **spin**!"

"The papyrus doesn't say anything about it, does it, Professor?" Colette asked.

He consulted the papyrus. "Hmm . . . I don't see anything. Nothing obvious, anyway."

"Let's not drag our paws," Nicky said. "Violet was right about the boulder. I say we TRUST her instincts! Let's try to push this giant wheel, too, and see what happens."

So everyone grabbed the POSTS that were sticking out of the wheel and started to push.

The first time they tried, nothing happened.

The second time they tried, the WHEEL almost moved, but then it seemed to get stuck.

The third time they tried, they **PUSHED** on the posts with all their might, and finally the wheel began to move! It moved little by little, very 𝕊𝕃𝕆𝕎𝕃𝕐, but steadily.

The mouselets and Professor Sparkle were working so **HARD** they didn't realize what was happening just a few feet below them.

From the side of the balcony, triangular slabs of stone were **OPENING** into the shape of a sail. They formed a small walkway. When the walkway was completely open, it **locked** into a stone pillar on the opposite side.

CRRRRRACK!

They'd made a bridge across the pit!

"**Sizzling spark plugs**, we did it!" shouted Pamela, who was the first to notice this **amazing** bridge. She pulled Violet into a hug and lifted her paws off the ground.

The slabs of stone form a bridge!

"You're the real cheese, sister!"

Back at the camp, Dunya was more excited than a mouseling on Christmouse morning. "Finally! They did it! LET'S GO get the treasure!" she SHOUTED.

THE TREASURE OF
THE SUN

Professor Sparkle wanted to cross the **BRIDGE** first, all by himself, to make sure it was safe. As soon as he'd reached the ledge on the other side, he called out to the Thea Sisters, "Come on, **MOUSELETS**! It's solid!"

Pamela didn't need to be asked twice. She crossed the bridge *QUICKER* than the mouse who ran up the clock. She was all the way on the other side when she remembered that Violet was afraid of **HEIGHTS**.

She turned around to find her friend very pale in the snout. Violet had stopped at the edge of the bridge, and the others were trying to **encourage** her to cross.

"You go," Violet pleaded. "I'll never be

able to do it. That pit . . . there's not even a railing. . . . I'll wait for you back here."

"Don't talk like that, Vi," Pam replied as she turned **BACK**. "You're the smartest of all of us, and you have the right to see the **treasure** first!"

The others agreed: If it hadn't been for Violet, they would never have moved the **BOULDER** from the entrance to the tunnel.

"Stay between Pam and me," Nicky suggested. "We'll hold your paws **TIGHTLY**, and we'll lead you across so you can close your eyes and not **LOOK** down."

Thanks to her friends, Violet managed to cross the bridge without looking into the **EMPTINESS** beneath her.

Once all the mouselets joined Professor Sparkle on the other side, they **scampered** through the doorway into a tunnel.

It was low and dark, but the torches cast **light** all around them. When the narrow passage opened up, all six mice found themselves covered in a cloud of golden dust.

COUGH! COUGH! COUGH!

Little by little, the dust settled and came to rest on the ground, where they saw . . .

THE TREASURE OF THE SUN!

The ship was huge, covered in gold, and filled with treasure!

Professor Sparkle and the Thea Sisters approached this **wonder** in silence, on tiptoe, as if they were **AFRAID** of disturbing a sacred place. After all, they were the first to **enter** this space in thousands of years!

Everything was intact, just as the pharaoh had left it. The **PAINTED** stone statues were imposing creatures with animal heads. Their glass eyes seemed to stare at the mouselets **STERNLY**.

Everywhere they looked, the mouselets and the **PROFESSOR** discovered beautiful works of art and treasure. It was a true **wonder** of the past, amazingly preserved for millennia!

They were still feeling shocked at their discovery when . . .

THUMP THUMP THUMP

. . . the far-off sound of hurried pawsteps awakened them from their trance.

"Dunya!" Professor Sparkle flinched, shivering, as if he had woken from a beautiful dream and fallen into a **NIGHTMARE**.

"They're **COMING** . . . ," Paulina whispered.

"What should we do?" Colette cried.

PAWS OFF!

Dunya and her henchmice didn't have any trouble **reaching** the Treasure of the Sun, since the Thea Sisters and Professor Sparkle had already cleared all the obstacles from the path. They burst into the room, **YELLING** and grabbing everything they could carry off by paw.

Professor Sparkle was **horrified**. "**ENOUGH!**" he shouted. "PAWS OFF! THESE ARE VERY DELICATE OBJECTS!"

Only when they had their paws on a huge amount of gold and jewels did the thieves finally calm down.

"Now we need to take it all out," Dunya commanded. "But be careful! If anyone **damages** any of this treasure, they'll have to answer to me!"

"What about the GOLDEN ship?" Tim asked. "We can't take it out of here in one piece."

Dunya thought for a moment, and then shrugged. "It's a shame, but we'll have to take it apart."

"NEVER!" Professor Sparkle interrupted, throwing himself in front of the ship to protect it. "I won't let you commit such a **crime** against archaeology!"

The Thea Sisters lined up next to him. They were ready for a **fight**.

"Don't you dare put your dirty paws on this treasure!" Paulina ordered.

Dunya laughed, **annoyed**, and turned her back to them. "Get them out of my way!" she ordered her henchmice. "I don't have time to waste on this bunch of drama rodents!"

Tim pushed Professor Sparkle to try to *MOVE* him, but the professor resisted, and the two tumbled to the ground. Soon they were wrestling.

Meanwhile, PAMELA, *Nicky*, PAULINA, *Colette*, and **Violet** had their paws full dealing with the other thieves. The mouselets **scurried** this way and that to resist Dunya's henchmice!

Finally, Professor Sparkle and Tim, still
LOCKED in their fight, rolled into a pyramid
of terra-cotta jars. The pyramid collapsed,
and the jars rolled every which way, knocking
into the Thea Sisters and making them
TOPPLE OVER like bowling pins.

"Get them, you **cheeseheads**!" Dunya
screamed at her henchmice. "Tie them up
and throw them in the next tunnel so they
won't get in the way of our **WORK**!"

Tim and the others obeyed. They grabbed

the Thea Sisters and Professor Sparkle and tossed them down a side corridor. Then

Dunya's henchmice blocked the entrance with a **large** statue.

THUNK!

The Thea Sisters and Professor Sparkle were shut up in the **DARK** without their cell phones or any other means to call for help.

Fortunately, Tim hadn't spent too much time tying them up, and all six managed to loosen their **CORDS** quicker than a cat with a ball of yarn. Unfortunately, they were still **TRAPPED** like rats in a maze!

CAUGHT in this narrow place without any light, Nicky started to panic.

"Come over here next to me," Colette told her friend. "I feel a little draft behind me."

Colette was right. A **light** air current was filtering through the stones in the wall. Nicky took a deep breath and tried to calm down. Then, when she felt more relaxed, she realized something.

"Listen, mouselets!" she whispered to her friends. "If **aiR** is coming through here, maybe we can move these stones and escape!"

The mouselets scratched at the walls with their paws. Soon, they'd dislodged a few pebbles. The stream of air became much **STRONGER**.

"There must be a **PASSAGEWAY**!" Pam exclaimed.

Professor Sparkle agreed. All six mice

emptied their pockets in search of things they could use to dig. They found two pens, a PENCIL, and a metal paper clip. Colette contributed a nail file, tweezers, and a few FUR PINS.

With a lot of **effort**, using the few tools they had, they managed to make the H O L E in the wall large enough to pass through it. On the other side, they discovered a tunnel that led upward.

"If air is coming through, this passage must reach the outside," Violet observed hopefully. Then she turned to Nicky. "Do you think you can crawl through there with us?"

Her friend nodded her snout **VIGOROUSLY**. "Anything to get out of here!"

ESCAPE!

The Thea Sisters and **Professor Sparkle** followed the long, narrow uphill passage until they emerged a short distance from the encampment. It was almost dawn. The six rodents stayed hidden behind some large **ROCKS**. For a few moments, they didn't squeak or move.

While they were catching their **breath**, taking in the cool morning air, they glimpsed the thieves **scurrying** back and forth. Dunya and her henchmice were preparing to remove the **treasure** from its underground hideaway.

Pamela pointed to a van a short distance away. "We can *escape* using that!" she whispered.

Professor Sparkle shook his snout. "They would catch us. Plus, we don't have the keys."

"Leave that to me, Professor," Pam replied. "I've learned a lot of useful things from my brother Sam, who's a **MECHANIC**!"

Professor Sparkle looked doubtful, but Paulina reassured him. "There isn't a motor in the world that can resist *PAm*!"

It took her only a few minutes. Pamela silently fiddled with the van's engine until she heard it RUMBLE: VRRRRMMMM.

The professor and the Thea Sisters jumped into the van and took off at top speed. The thieves immediately caught sight of their prisoners **RACING** off right under their snouts, and they were left squeakless.

"**Follow them, you tail twirlers!!!**" Dunya screamed.

Every SUV in the camp was sent out on the chase.

EVERYBODY FREEZE!

As a driver, Pamela proved to be worth her weight in cheese. It was truly a **legendary** undertaking to guide the van over the desert terrain, over stones and **POTHOLES**, without hitting the rocky canyon walls, turning over the van, or even popping a **tire**!

Unfortunately, Dunya's **SUV** was faster than the van, in part because it wasn't carrying as many rodents.

As the van bounced over mile after mile of sandy terrain, the Thea Sisters watched their **PURSUERS** gain on them. "Can't this rat trap go any quicker?" Nicky asked in desperation.

Pam gritted her teeth. "Sorry, Nicky! If I go any faster, we'll **roll** over like a ball of mozzarella."

Finally, they caught sight of a dirt trail. It had to be the way to Luxor.

But just at that moment, a **RED** light appeared on the dashboard. "Oh, no!" Pam groaned with **DESPAIR**. "We're out of gas!"

They continued on, but without gas they were **DONE FOR**. The van would stop pretty soon, and who would be able to help them in this **REMOTE** place?

"Hey! I see a cloud of dust over there!" Violet exclaimed, pointing in front of them. "Maybe it's a bus!"

But Nicky and Colette, who were keeping track of their pursuers, **SHOUTED**, "Keep going, Pam! Dunya's SUV is right behind us! **GO, GO, GO!!!**"

RRRNNNN ...PUTT ...PUTT ...PUTT ...

The van sputtered and came to a stop.

Pamela abandoned the wheel with a sigh. "Well, at least we tried!"

It was no more than a moment or two before Dunya's henchmice reached them.

Tim yanked the mouselets and the professor out of the van. He was furious.

"GET OUT HERE! PAWS UP! NOW I'LL SHOW YOU, YOU FILTHY, ROTTEN CHEESES!"

Dunya scurried over to Professor Sparkle and **sneered**, "Well done, Bart! You almost managed to **escape**!"

But her smile turned into a grimace when a gruff squeak called out, "**POLICE! EVERYBODY FREEZE!**"

MARiA SOUNDS
THE ALARM

The cloud of dust Violet had seen on the **horizon** wasn't a bus; it was an SUV that belonged to the Egyptian **POLICE**, who were out searching for them!

The officers had arrived just in time. Caught by surprise, Dunya, Tim, and their henchmice were forced to give themselves up.

Leaving the **CRiMiNALS** to his officers, the police chief turned to the Thea Sisters. "Is there a Paulina here?"

Paulina **JUMPED** up and came forward timidly. "Um, that's me. . . . Why?"

The policeman **SMiLeD** and pawed her a cell phone. "Give your little sister a call, miss! She's moved **mountains** of cheese to get us to find you!"

"**MARIA?!?**" the Thea Sisters exclaimed.

It seems incredible, doesn't it? But here's what happened:

The arrival of the police **saved** the Thea

Sniff sniff!

Sisters and Professor Sparkle just when they had given up their last **hope**. But the police got involved only because of little Maria, all the way on the **OPPOSITE** side of the world!

Paulina and Maria had long video chats on the **Internet** every evening. When her sister didn't contact her for a few days, Maria became **ALARMED**, and she called me, Thea Stilton.

I knew at once that something was amiss. Paulina would never fail to contact Maria unless something was seriously wrong. So I contacted a dear **friend** who is a journalist in Cairo, and she got in touch with the police in Luxor!

"Way to go, Maria!" Paulina exclaimed. She was extremely proud of her little sister.

"FRIENDS TOGETHER! MICE FOREVER!" Nicky, Violet, Pamela, and Colette cried.

"I questioned Professor Mouserson at his dig," the police official explained. "He told me that you had gone to an area southwest of the Nile. And he added that you had taken an ancient papyrus and a priceless lapis lazuli scarab!"

Professor Sparkle decided that this was the moment to squeak up. "These rotten rodents are plunderers!" he explained to the official. "They wanted to break

apart the Treasure of the Sun so that they could sell the gold!"

He led the police officers back to the site of their discovery. When they **ARRIVED** at the camp and the chief saw the trunks full of **PRECIOUS ARTIFACTS**, he immediately called headquarters: "I need backup!" He and the other police officers were determined

HOLY SPHINX SNOUTS!

to preserve the **treasure** and protect the archaeological site from thieves.

"There's an **ENORMOUSE** amount of cataloging to be done here!" Professor Sparkle told the mouselets. "A detailed list of all the artifacts must be made iMMEDiATELY, before anything DISAPPEARS!"

"Well, it's about time," Nicky said, winking. "That's what we came for, isn't it? Not for an **ADVENTURE** . . . just to catalog artifacts!"

Everyone **burst** out laughing.

GREAT JOB, MARIA!

A few weeks after this incredible ADVENTURE, Maria and I arrived at the Luxor airport. It was two o'clock in the **afternoon**, the hottest time of day in Egypt.

I was a little tired after the long flight. Maria, on the other paw, had spent twice as much time on an airplane as I had, since she had come all the way from Peru — but she was *buzzing* around like a bee in a field of **flowers**!

When she saw Paulina waiting for her at the baggage claim, she leaped into her sister's paws. They both would have fallen to the **GROUND** if the other Thea Sisters hadn't been there, ready to catch them!

Maria and Paulina covered each other with

KISSES. They were so happy to see each other they forgot everyone else was there. I knew I was better off asking the other mouselets when the exhibition would begin.

"Moldy Brie on baguettes, that's been the hardest part of the whole adventure," Colette replied. "Moving things from here to there, being careful about the lights, and setting up!"

"Poor Colette has broken every pawnail she has," Nicky said teasingly. "You can imagine the *stress*!"

"It's been a bit of a challenge," Violet said. "But in the end, the exhibition turned out **beautifully**! You'll see at the opening."

We went straight to the hotel. Maria and I needed to shower and then get dressed up for the opening ceremony.

Paulina had bought a new dress for her little SISTER, who had been named the guest of honor. "You'll be the one to cut the ribbon at the ceremony!" she promised Maria, who was very nervous about it.

"But why me?" she asked, **blushing**. "You and the other Thea Sisters are the ones who found the Treasure of the Sun!"

"But you *are* a Thea Sister!"* Pamela reminded her, and the others applauded in agreement.

CLAP! CLAP! CLAP!

"Besides," Violet added, "if it weren't for you, the Treasure of the Sun would have been reduced to a million tiny little **PIECES** by now!"

---

* Do you remember? In my book *Thea Stilton and the Secret City*, Maria became a Thea Sister!

Maria smiled shyly.

Soon we were all ready. We headed for the mouseum. I was very curious to see the exhibition. Plus I wanted to interview all the characters in this **amazing** adventure. So I asked Colette, "Will Professor Mouserson be there?"

She shrugged and **SIGHED**. "Who knows? It was a real BLOW to him that

Professor Sparkle was the one to find the **TREASURE OF THE SUN**."

But when we arrived at the exhibition, we had a pleasant **SURPRISE**: The two professors were chatting away like old friends. Professor Sparkle insisted that the great **Egyptologist** stand next to him in the official photo.

"Without his papyrus and the lapis lazuli

scarab, I never would have found the Treasure of the Sun!" he said sincerely.

The Thea Sisters and I preferred to pose for a **PHOTO** that was much less *formal*, in front of the Treasure of the Sun. For us, the most important part of this **ADVENTURE** was getting to be together again!

THEY WERE MORE THAN FRIENDS. THEY WERE SISTERS!

Thea Sisters

Don't miss any of my other fabumouse adventures!

Thea Stilton and the Dragon's Code

Thea Stilton and the Mountain of Fire

Thea Stilton and the Ghost of the Shipwreck

Thea Stilton and the Secret City

Thea Stilton and the Mystery in Paris

Thea Stilton and the Cherry Blossom Adventure

Thea Stilton and the Star Castaways

Thea Stilton: Big Trouble in the Big Apple

Thea Stilton and the Ice Treasure

Thea Stilton and the Secret of the Old Castle

Want to read my next adventure?
I can't wait to tell you all about it!

THIS HOTEL IS HAUNTED

My good friend Hercule Poirat and I were called to investigate mysterious events in the famouse Grand Hotel in New Mouse City. There was a ghost haunting the hotel and scaring guests! It was wearing armor and carrying a ball and chain. I know that ghosts don't exist, but this was pretty spooky. Would Poirat and I be able to solve this spine-tingling mystery?

Be sure to read these stories, too!

#1 Lost Treasure of the Emerald Eye

#2 The Curse of the Cheese Pyramid

#3 Cat and Mouse in a Haunted House

#4 I'm Too Fond of My Fur!

#5 Four Mice Deep in the Jungle

#6 Paws Off, Cheddarface!

#7 Red Pizzas for a Blue Count

#8 Attack of the Bandit Cats

#9 A Fabumouse Vacation for Geronimo

#10 All Because of a Cup of Coffee

#11 It's Halloween, You 'Fraidy Mouse!

#12 Merry Christmas, Geronimo!

#13 The Phantom of the Subway

#14 The Temple of the Ruby of Fire

#15 The Mona Mousa Code

#16 A Cheese-Colored Camper

#17 Watch Your Whiskers, Stilton!

#18 Shipwreck on the Pirate Islands

#19 My Name Is Stilton, Geronimo Stilton

#20 Surf's Up, Geronimo!

#21 The Wild, Wild West

#22 The Secret of Cacklefur Castle

A Christmas Tale

#23 Valentine's Day Disaster

#24 Field Trip to Niagara Falls

#25 The Search for Sunken Treasure

#26 The Mummy with No Name

#27 The Christmas Toy Factory

#28 Wedding Crasher

#29 Down and Out Down Under

#30 The Mouse Island Marathon

#31 The Mysterious Cheese Thief

Christmas Catastrophe

#32 Valley of the Giant Skeletons

#33 Geronimo and the Gold Medal Mystery

#34 Geronimo Stilton, Secret Agent

#35 A Very Merry Christmas

#36 Geronimo's Valentine

#37 The Race Across America

#38 A Fabumouse School Adventure

#39 Singing Sensation

#40 The Karate Mouse

#41 Mighty Mount Kilimanjaro

#42 The Peculiar Pumpkin Thief

#43 I'm Not a Supermouse!

#44 The Giant Diamond Robbery

#45 Save the White Whale!

#46 The Haunted Castle

#47 Run for the Hills, Geronimo!

#48 The Mystery in Venice

#49 The Way of the Samurai

And coming soon!

#50 This Hotel Is Haunted!

Meet
CREEPELLA VON CACKLEFUR

I, *Geronimo Stilton*, have a lot of mouse friends, but none as **spooky** as my friend CREEPELLA VON CACKLEFUR! She is an enchanting and MYSTERIOUS mouse with a pet bat named Bitewing. YIKES! I'm a real 'fraidy mouse, but even I think CREEPELLA and her family are AWFULLY fascinating. I can't wait for you to read all about CREEPELLA in these fa-mouse-ly funny and **spectacularly spooky** tales!

#1 The Thirteen Ghosts

#2 Meet Me in Horrorwood

#3 Ghost Pirate Treasure

THANKS FOR READING, AND GOOD-BYE UNTIL OUR NEXT ADVENTURE!

TheaSisters